Dear Parents, Educators, and Guardians,

Thank you for helping your child dive into this book with us. We believe in the power of books to transport readers to other worlds, expand their horizons, and help them discover cultures and experiences that may differ from their own.

We also believe that books should inspire young readers to imagine a diverse world that includes them, a world in which they can see themselves as the heroes of their own stories.

These are our hopes for *all* our readers. So come on. Dive into reading and explore the world with us!

Best wishes,
Your friends at Lee & Low

The Protest

Henry   Lily   Mei   Pablo   Padma

by **Samantha Thornhill**

illustrated by **Shirley Ng-Benitez**

Lee & Low Books Inc.   New York

Dedicated to the dreamers —S.T.

To the Benitez family, and to friends everywhere
who peacefully assemble for the rights
of the greater good —S.N-B.

LEE & LOW BOOKS Inc., 95 Madison Avenue, New York, NY 10016, leeandlow.com
Book design by Charice Silverman
Book production by The Kids at Our House
The illustrations are rendered in watercolor and altered digitally
Manufactured in China by Imago
Printed on paper from responsible sources
(hc) 10 9 8 7 6 5 4 3 2 1
(pb) 10 9 8 7 6 5 4 3 2 1
First Edition

Library of Congress Cataloging-in-Publication Data
Names: Thornhill, Samantha, author. | Ng-Benitez, Shirley, illustrator.
Title: The protest / by Samantha Thornhill; illustrated by Shirley Ng-Benitez.
Description: First edition. | New York: Lee & Low Books, [2021]
Series: Dive into reading! | Audience: Ages 4-7. | Audience: Grades K-1.
Summary: "Lily and her friends organize a protest in order to save their
neighborhood public garden from being demolished" —Provided by publisher.
Identifiers: LCCN 2020021772 | ISBN 9781643792088 (hardcover)
ISBN 9781643792095 (paperback) | ISBN 9781643794730 (ebook)
Subjects: CYAC: Protest movements—Fiction. | Community gardens—Fiction.
Classification: LCC PZ7.T3934 Pr 2020 | DDC [E]—dc23
LC record available at https://lccn.loc.gov/2020021772

Contents

Bad News   4

Bright Ideas   14

Rally Day   22

Bad News

Lily and her mom walked
to the public garden to see
their neighbor Mr. Sam.

Mr. Sam was not watering
the plants as usual.

"Are you okay, Mr. Sam?"
asked Lily.
"No," said Mr. Sam.

"We have to close our garden.
Some builders want to make our
public garden into a parking lot."

"The city is changing fast
with new people and buildings,"
said Mr. Sam.
Lily frowned and looked around.

It wasn't fair to close
the public garden.
"Can we save the garden?"
asked Lily.
"We can try," said Mr. Sam.

Lily shared the news with her friends
Padma, Pablo, Mei, and Henry.
"What will we do after school
without the garden?" asked Mei.

"Where will our school get
vegetables for lunch?" asked Padma.
"Where will I get strawberries
for breakfast?" asked Pablo.

"We need to protest the closing
of the garden," said Lily.
"But we're just kids!" said Henry.

"Hey, we *kids* grew enough
vegetables to feed our school
at lunch," said Padma.
"Kids can do a lot!" said Lily.

Bright Ideas

Lily thought about how to protest. People could call their neighbors. People could make posters.

People could invite reporters.
Lily decided to plan a rally
to save the garden.

Lily shared her plan for a rally
with her friends and parents.
"Good idea, Lily!" they said.
They planned to hold the rally
in one week.

Lily and her friends told
their neighbors about the rally.
Together they would protest
the closing of the garden.

Then the friends met at Lily's home
to make posters for the protest.
Henry brought poster boards.
Pablo brought rulers.

Mei brought markers and glitter glues.
Padma and Lily thought about
what to write on the posters.

After they finished the posters,
they needed a chant.
"What should we say?" asked Mei.
"No cars, no! Let our garden
grow!" said Lily.

No cars, no!
Let our
garden grow!

"Great chant, Lily!" said Henry.
Now they were ready for the rally.
Lily hoped others would join them.

Rally Day

On the morning of the rally,
Lily, her friends, and their parents
waited outside their building.

It looked as if no one else
was coming to protest.

But then neighbors, kids from school, and their parents came to protest.

Lily and her friends were happy.

Everyone started walking
to the garden together.
Everyone held their posters high.
"No cars, no! Let our garden
grow!" everyone chanted.

More neighbors joined the protest.
The crowd grew larger.
The chant grew louder.

Finally everyone arrived
at the garden.
A reporter came to the rally.
The reporter asked Lily
about the protest.

Then Mr. Sam got a phone call.
The crowd became quiet
and listened.

Mr. Sam said the builders would
wait until next year to build
the parking lot.
The people had saved the garden!

The crowd cheered.
"When they try to turn our garden
into a parking lot again,
we will be ready!" said Lily.

☆ **Activity** ☆

🍎 Think about a place in your community that is special to you, such as the library, park, or museum. Write down why it's important to you. Why do you like going there?

🍎 Find out how places in your community need help. Does the library have to replace books? Does trash need to be picked up at the park?

🍎 Then make posters or signs encouraging classmates or neighbors to come together and help out those places in your community. You could hold a bake sale to raise money for the local library or have a "pick up trash" day.

Samantha Thornhill is a poet and an author of children's books. As an educator, she has taught poetry to acting students at the Juilliard School and creative writing seminars at the Bronx Academy of Letters. Samantha is a native of the twin-island nation of Trinidad and Tobago and currently lives in Brooklyn, NY. You can learn more about her at samanthaspeaks.com.

Shirley Ng-Benitez loves to draw and write. She creates her art with watercolor, gouache, pencil, and digital techniques. She lives in the Bay Area of California and is inspired by nature, her family, her pup, and her two kittens. Visit her online at shirleyngbenitez.com.

Read More About Lily and Her Friends!